This book belongs to ★

....

....

....

ARION and the DOLPHIN

To the wild Irish dolphin, "Fungie" V.S.
To David J.R.

This book is based on the libretto written by Vikram Seth for the opera *Arion and the Dolphin*, composed by Alec Roth. The opera was commissioned by the Baylis Programme of English National Opera and was first performed in Plymouth in June 1994.

The video of *The Story of Arion and the Dolphin*, as seen on Channel Four, is available from Grasshopper Enterprises, 50 Peel Street, London, W8 7PD.

Published as a Dolphin Paperback in 1997
First published in Great Britain in 1994
by Orion Children's Books
a division of the Orion Publishing Group Ltd
Orion House
5 Upper St Martin's Lane
London WC2H 9EA

A catalogue record for this book is available from the British Library

Printed in Italy

ISBN 1 85881 430 8

·ARION· and·the· ·DOLPHIN·

·by Vikram Seth·
·illustrated by·
·Jane·Ray·

Dolphin

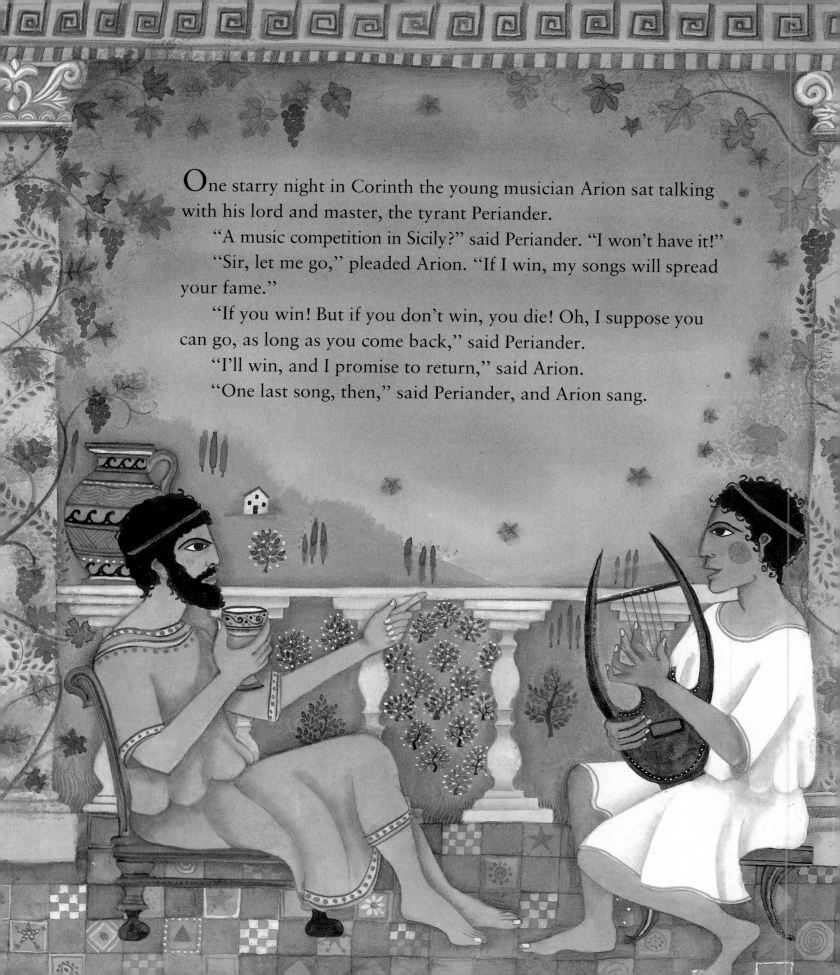

One starry night in Corinth the young musician Arion sat talking with his lord and master, the tyrant Periander.

"A music competition in Sicily?" said Periander. "I won't have it!"

"Sir, let me go," pleaded Arion. "If I win, my songs will spread your fame."

"If you win! But if you don't win, you die! Oh, I suppose you can go, as long as you come back," said Periander.

"I'll win, and I promise to return," said Arion.

"One last song, then," said Periander, and Arion sang.

Bright stars, guide me to fame
By land, by sea –
So that my form and name
May rest among you in the sky –
And you, dark restless sea,
Be gentle on my way
From Greece to Sicily.

Arion set sail for Sicily. He talked to the ship's Captain, who was glad to have him for company, and listened to the sailors singing as they worked.

Our decks are scrubbed and clean –
sang the sailors,
Our ropes run strong and free.
Fair winds, fill out our sails –
Bring us no gusts or gales –
Keep us from sharks and whales
From Greece to Sicily.

"Arion! Let's hear you sing!" shouted one of the sailors, and Arion joined in.

> *Dark restless sea,*
> *Blue, green, black, grey –*
> *Be gentle on my way*
> *From Greece to Sicily.*
> *May no storm shake the sky,*
> *Or seagulls wheel and cry,*
> *But dolphins dip and fly*
> *Beside my ship and me.*

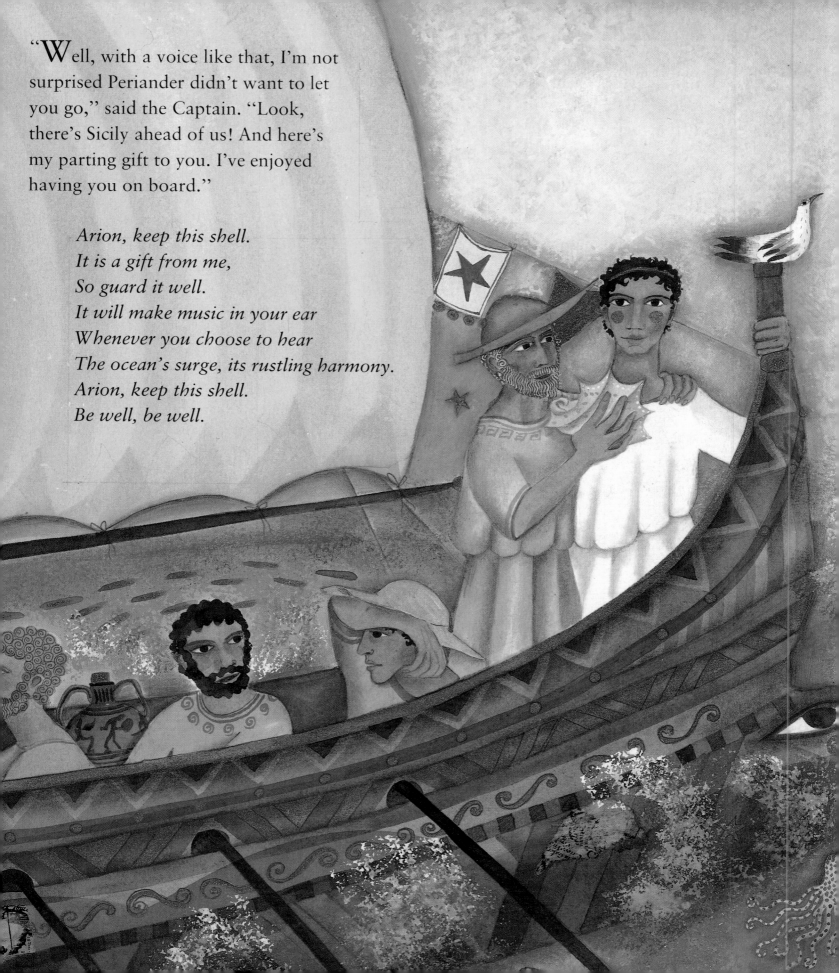

"Well, with a voice like that, I'm not surprised Periander didn't want to let you go," said the Captain. "Look, there's Sicily ahead of us! And here's my parting gift to you. I've enjoyed having you on board."

Arion, keep this shell.
It is a gift from me,
So guard it well.
It will make music in your ear
Whenever you choose to hear
The ocean's surge, its rustling harmony.
Arion, keep this shell.
Be well, be well.

Crowds thronged the harbour to see the ship.
"Who've you got on board?" someone shouted.

"The winner of your competition, for one!"
said the Captain. "Arion will teach you Sicilians
how to sing. Arion, my friend, I must leave you.
I will come back later to take you home to
Corinth."

"Let's give him a good time!" said one of the
Sicilians. Arion was pleased. There was plenty of
time to practise before the competition.

But there was no practising. Arion spent his time feasting and drinking, enjoying his freedom. When at last he stood up to sing, not a sound came out.

"Two false starts is all you get!" said the master of ceremonies.

Despairing, Arion remembered the shell. He put it to his ear and heard the surge of the sea. Softly he began to sing, and as his song grew stronger and sweeter the Sicilians shouted, "More! More! Arion is the winner!"

Arion accepted his prize of gold. It was time
to leave. He sang one last song:

Dark, restless sea
Accept my weight once more
As gently as before.
Bear me to Corinth shore
Alive, and safe, and free.

Back on board ship, Arion slept while the sailors grumbled to the Captain.

"Why should he have that gold? Let's take it!"

"No!" cried the Captain. "I will not touch that gold."

"We'll have the gold, or you die! Think of your wife and children . . ."

"Then, Arion, *you* must die!" said the Captain.
"I cannot see my family harmed."

"Spare me my life!" cried Arion, waking.
"I'll give you all my gold."

"No," said the Captain, "when we reach Corinth, you
will go back on your promise. You must jump overboard."

"Let me sing one last song," said Arion.

I do not wish to die. I fear to die,
To sink in the reflection of the sky,
At such a fearful depth to be alone,
To merge with shell and coral, slime and stone,
By tentacles caressed, by green fronds curled,
To drown myself in such a silent world.

O world so beautiful, grey olive trees,
Green laurel bushes, tempest-troubled seas,
I shall not see you or the clouds at night
Or the gold stars or sunset's golden light
Or smell the hyacinth or hear the cry
Of eagle or of wolf before I die.

Arion jumped into the sea.
The moon and stars
disappeared. There was
blackness. He was
drowning.

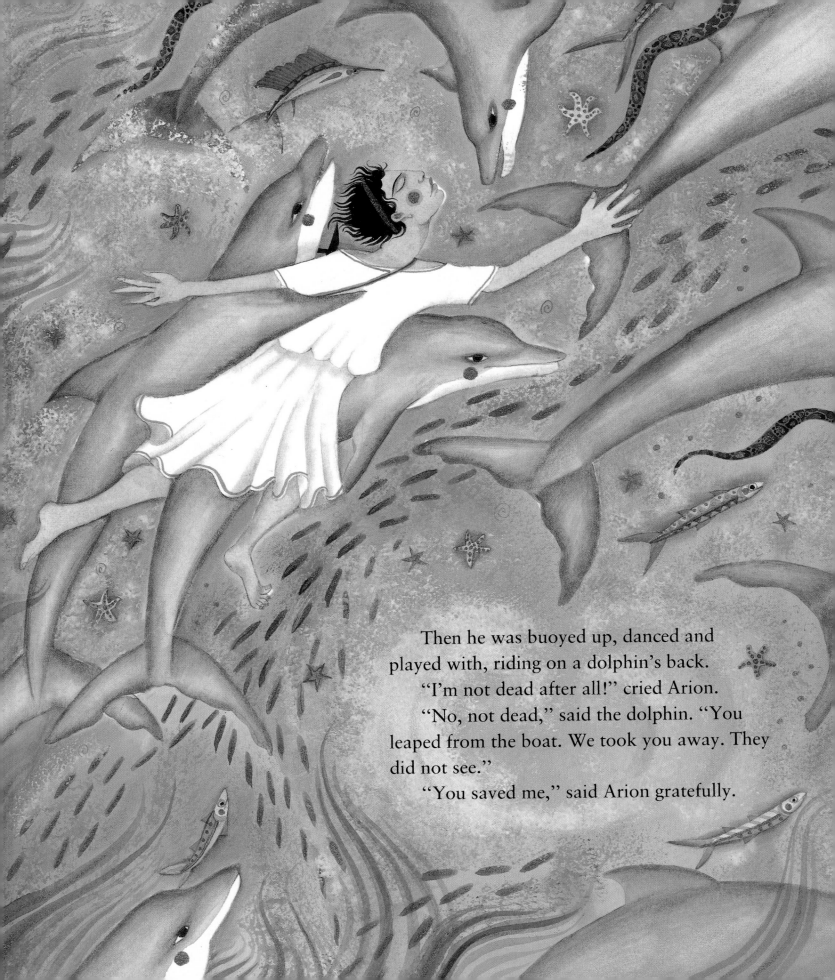

Then he was buoyed up, danced and played with, riding on a dolphin's back.

"I'm not dead after all!" cried Arion.

"No, not dead," said the dolphin. "You leaped from the boat. We took you away. They did not see."

"You saved me," said Arion gratefully.

"I'll take you home to Corinth," said the dolphin.
"But first it's time for supper!"
The dolphins began to catch and pass and
share fish. Arion watched entranced while they
played and sang their song.

> Fish give us a sufficiency
>   Beneath the sea
>   As you can see.
> We eat with great efficiency
>   Beneath the sea
>   As you can see.

> Our skins are smooth and rubbery
> Our bulky bodies blubbery.
> We harry herring happily
> And swallow salmon snappily.

"Let's sing a duet together," said the dolphin
to Arion when they had finished.

So Arion and the dolphin sang together. As they swam towards Corinth their voices intertwined.

> The days pass one by one
> > sang Arion
> I feel my life has only just begun —
> And, for the first time I am having fun!
>
> In air and water both, our voices part and blend,
> And I, who never sought a friend
> Have found one in the end.

The dolphin sang:

> I love Arion and would like to be
> Bound to his voice and him eternally.

The days passed, and they swam into the gulf of Corinth,
where fisherfolk crowded round to point and stare.

Now, dolphin, you must go,
said Arion
My part is here above, and yours below –
I where the winds, you where the waters flow.
It must be so.

But the dolphin did not want to leave Arion.

With you I will remain –
the dolphin sang
For if we part we'll never meet again
And I would die of loneliness and pain.
This I maintain.

"Look, it's Arion, riding on a dolphin!" yelled a fisherman. "Tell Periander!"

Periander came hurrying to embrace Arion.

"You won the competition? Where are your prizes? Why are you not with the Captain?"

"My lord, my friend the dolphin saved my life," said Arion, and he told his story and how the dolphin wanted to stay with him.

"Absurd!" said Periander. "The Captain is a highly trusted man. You're lying! And how do you know the dolphin wants to stay with you? Explain!"

"We spoke, my lord —" said Arion.

"You spoke? Then command it to speak now so that I may hear dolphin language too," said Periander. "If it speaks, throw it a mackerel. Speak now! Speak!"

But the dolphin was silent.

"Arrest him! He's lying!" roared Periander. The guards led Arion away.

"What about the dolphin, my lord?" asked a fisherman.

"Oh – do what you like with the dolphin!" snapped Periander.

The fisherfolk pushed and poked at the dolphin.
They caged it in a small pool and made people pay
to see it jump for dead fish.

Meanwhile, Arion was locked in a prison cell.
It was not long before a guard came to tell him the
dolphin was dead.

> *The dolphin wasted away*
> *From day to day*
> > said the guard
> *It glutted and it groaned.*
> *It squeaked, it moaned.*
> *"Arion . . . Arion . . ." all day long*
> *It seemed to say – a high, pathetic song.*
> *Into its misery the creature sank.*
> *Ringed by dead fish, it stank.*

Arion's cry of grief made Periander rush into
the cell.

"Forgive me, Arion! I should not have kept you
apart. I will build a tomb for the dolphin, and you
shall go free."

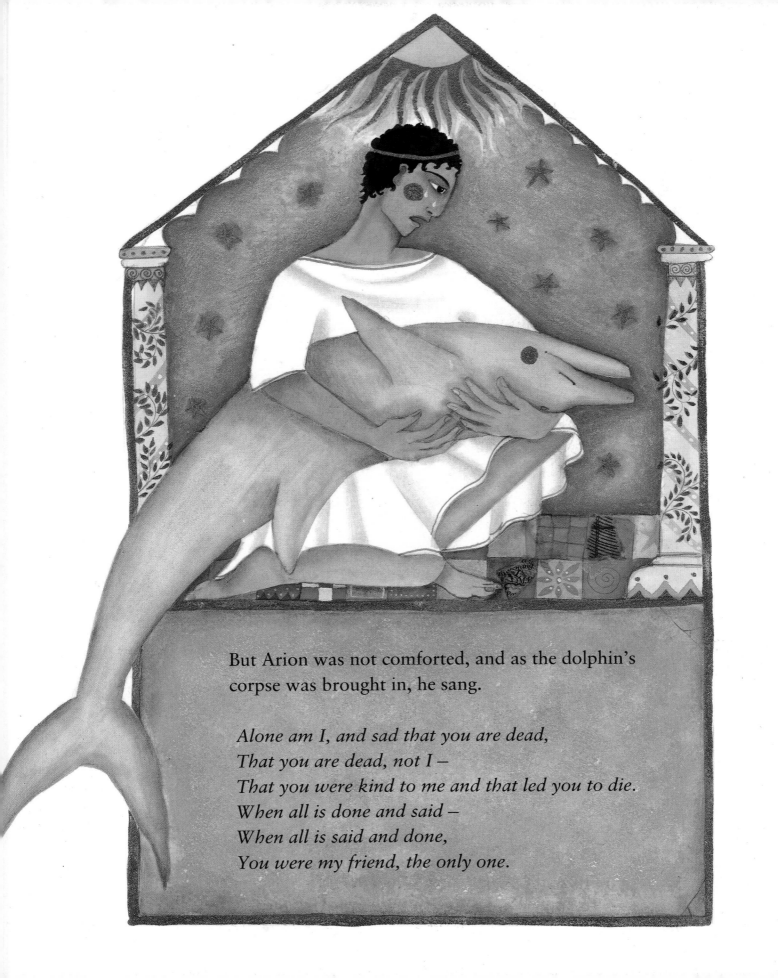

But Arion was not comforted, and as the dolphin's corpse was brought in, he sang.

Alone am I, and sad that you are dead,
That you are dead, not I —
That you were kind to me and that led you to die.
When all is done and said —
When all is said and done,
You were my friend, the only one.

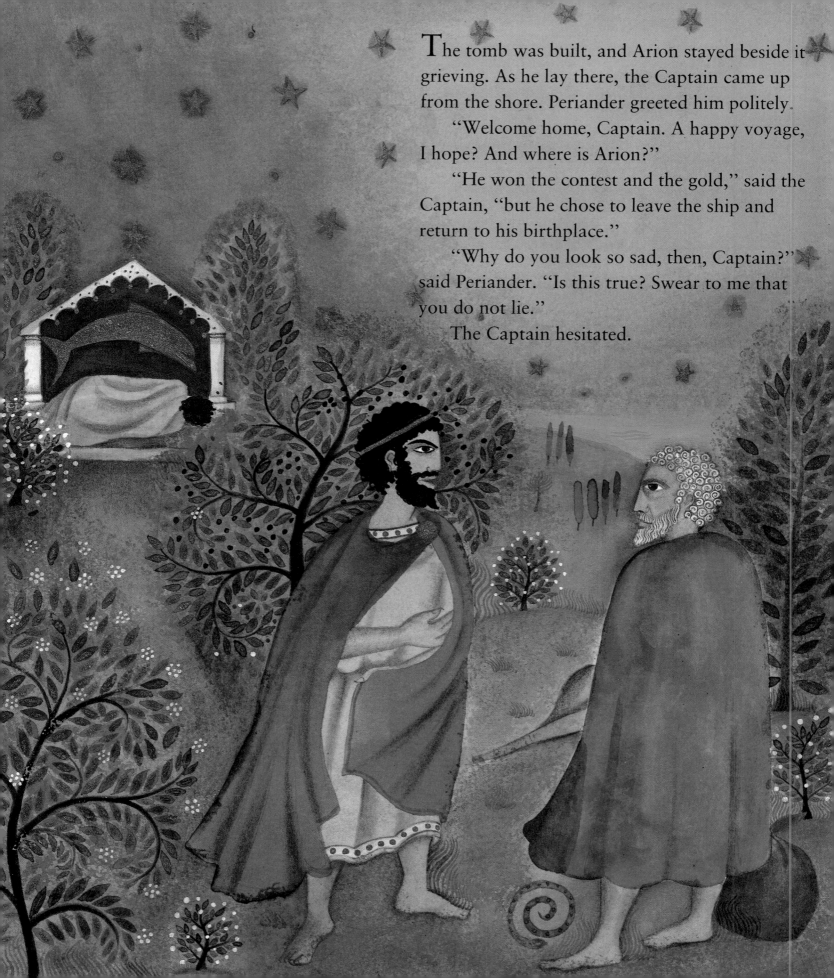

The tomb was built, and Arion stayed beside it
grieving. As he lay there, the Captain came up
from the shore. Periander greeted him politely.

"Welcome home, Captain. A happy voyage,
I hope? And where is Arion?"

"He won the contest and the gold," said the
Captain, "but he chose to leave the ship and
return to his birthplace."

"Why do you look so sad, then, Captain?"
said Periander. "Is this true? Swear to me that
you do not lie."

The Captain hesitated.

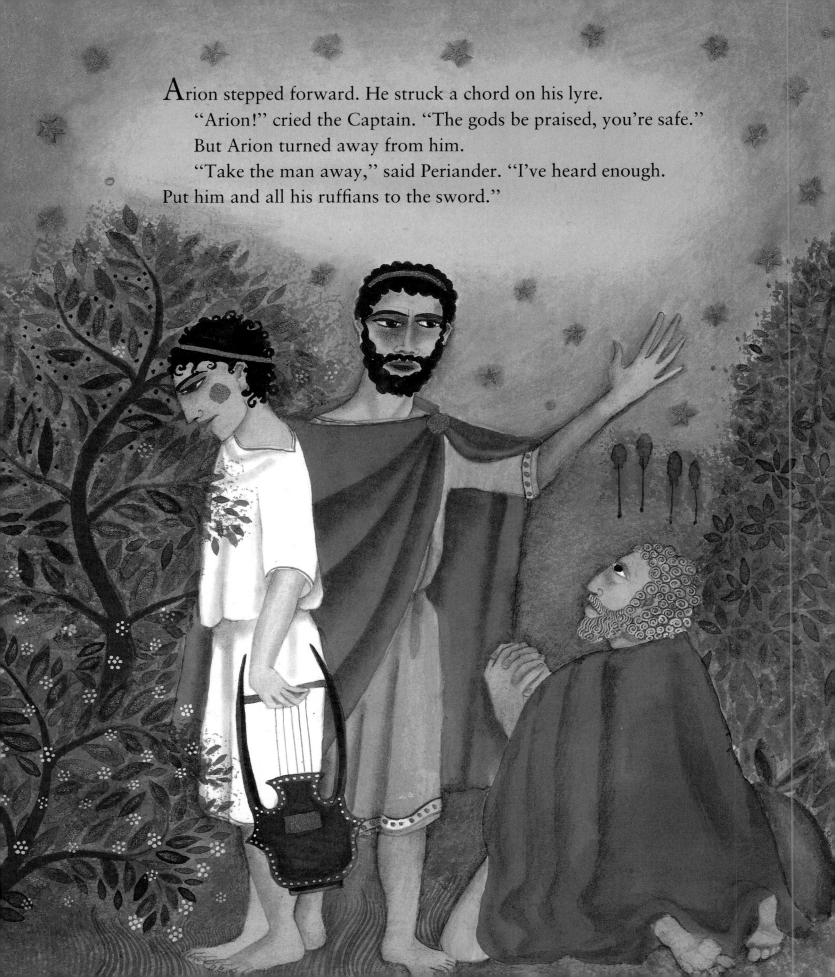

Arion stepped forward. He struck a chord on his lyre.
"Arion!" cried the Captain. "The gods be praised, you're safe."
But Arion turned away from him.
"Take the man away," said Periander. "I've heard enough.
Put him and all his ruffians to the sword."

"No, let them go, my lord," said Arion. "At least delay their sentence for an hour and let me play to you. Perhaps my words will ease this bitterness."

Periander nodded. "Play, then, and sing. I have caused you pain, but now I will listen."

Arion plucked at his lyre, and sang . . .

I hear your voice sing out my name by night,
By dawn, by evening light.

Dolphin, it was from your marine caress
That I learned gentleness.

Warm earth, teach us to nourish, not destroy
The souls that give us joy.

Bright stars, engrave my dolphin and my lyre
In the night sky with fire.